Watch Out for WOLFGANG

Paul Carrick

Charlesbridge

TO MY MOM, WHO THOUGHTFULLY
SUPPORTED HER TWO BOTS
IN FOLLOWING THEIR BLISS,
ENCOURAGING THEM TO BUILD
WHATEVER THEY WANTED

Published by Charlesbridge
85 Main Street
Watertown, MA 02472
(617) 926-0329
www.charlesbridge.com

Library of Congress Cataloging-in-Publication Data
Carrick, Paul.
    Watch out for Wolfgang / Paul Carrick.
        p. cm.
    Summary: When an old mother robot sends her three sons out into the world to
make their own way, the outcome is not what anyone expects.
    ISBN 978-1-57091-689-2 (reinforced for library use)
[1. Robots—Fiction.] I. Title.
PZ7.C2344Wat 2009
[E]—dc22   2008007246

Printed in Singapore
(hc) 10 9 8 7 6 5 4 3 2 1

Illustrations done in mixed media
Display type and text type set in Hoosker, designed by T-26, Chicago, IL
Color separations by Chroma Graphics, Singapore
Printed and bound by Imago
Production supervision by Brian G. Walker
Designed by Susan Mallory Sherman

Once upon a time an old mother robot

raised three sons: Rod, Slick, and Dudley. The bots could not have been more different.

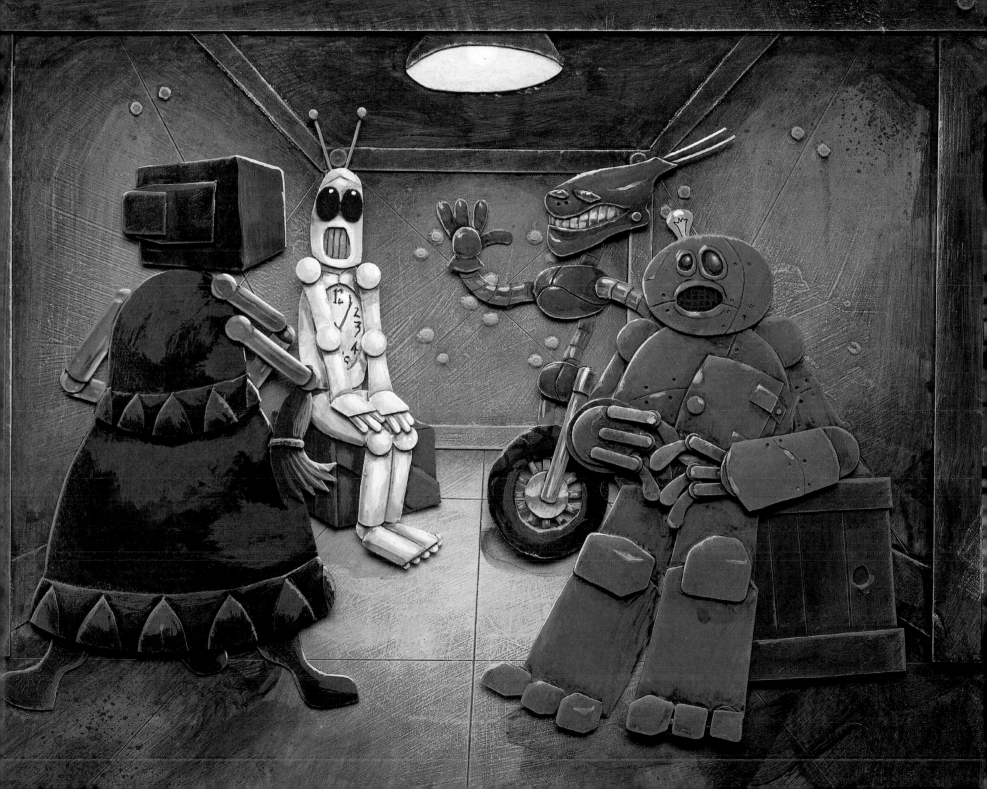

Rod cleaned his room, oiled his gears, and always polished his chrome before bedtime. He made his mother proud.

Life was easy for Slick. His smile, good looks, and sweet talk always got him what he wanted.

But no one seemed to understand Dudley. Dud, as his brothers called him, was rusty, made funny sounds, and had his own way of doing things. He was, in a word, odd.

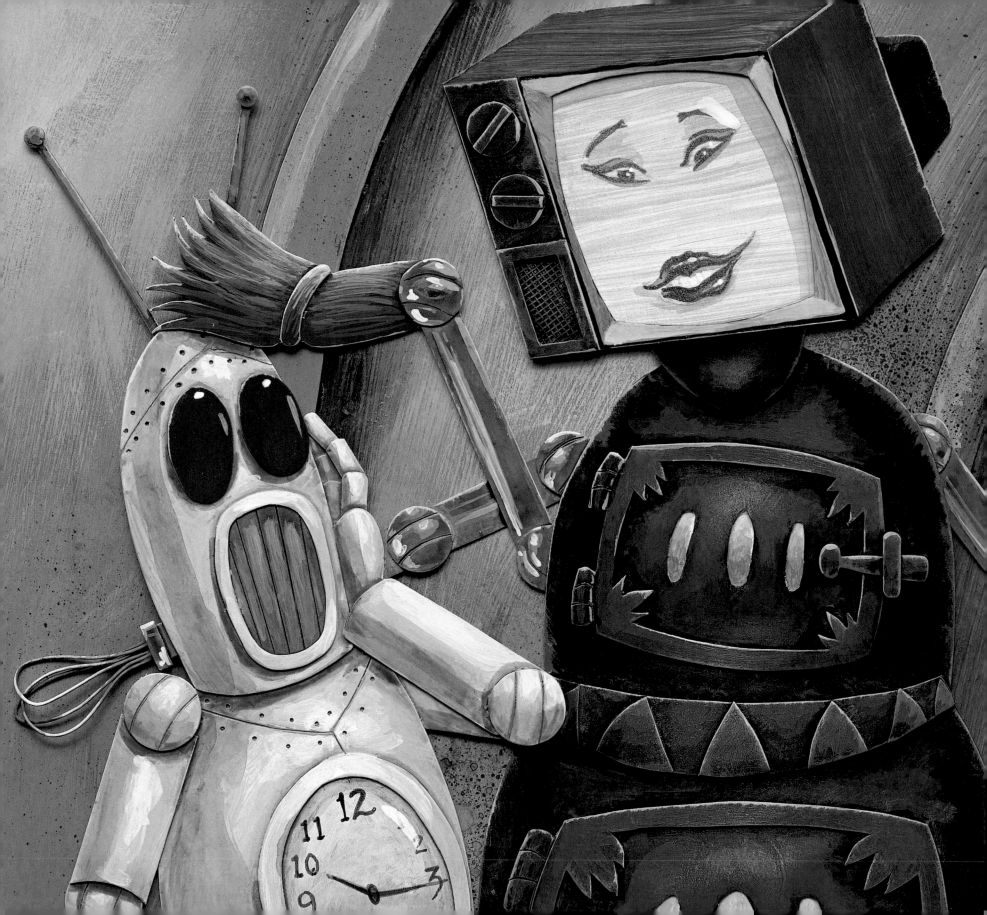

One day the old robot gathered her bots around her.

"Now that you're all finished being assembled,
it's time for each of you to go out on your own," she said.

"But Mother dear, where will we live?" asked Rod.

The old bot patted his head. "I've scrimped and saved,
Roddy, so that you and your brothers can have your own
factories. But you must build them big and strong to
keep out Wolfgang the Recycler. If he catches you,
who knows what he'll make from your parts! Toasters,
microwaves . . ." Her screen flickered frantically.

Rod shuddered with fear. "Thank you, Mother. I will
spend the money carefully and wisely."

"Hah! No problem, Mumsy," scoffed Slick. "I can handle old Wolfie!"

"You know BIP," said Dud dreamily, "I've always wanted to live in a h-u-u-ge pile of mud BEEP. I'd love to smell the smog from the smokestacks wafting in and feel the mud squish through my gears BUZZ."

The old robot sighed and rolled her eyes.

Rod snickered and said, "Don't waste your money, Dud. Follow your programming! Don't you want Mother to be proud of you?"

Slick shook his head. "You must have some bolts missing—and by the way, have you ever heard of chrome polish? Mumsy, are you sure he and I came from the same factory?"

The three bots kissed their mother
goodbye and set off with their money.
Rod bought a solid factory just like
his mother's. "I'm safe from Wolfgang
here," he thought, sweeping and
scrubbing until the place sparkled.

Slick went to the racetrack and gambled his mother's money. He won three times what she had given him. With his new fortune he built a custom-made, reinforced-steel castle, full of all the latest gadgets.

"I'd like to see that Wolfie try to get into my house," he chuckled.

Dudley knew exactly what he wanted. He ordered mud—
heaping piles of it.

When twelve truckloads of the sloppiest muck were dumped
in his yard, Dud's lightbulb popped with delight.

"How grand BUZZ BIP!" Dudley jumped into the mud
with a huge splash. He couldn't have been happier.

Wolfgang was gleeful when he learned of his three
new neighbors. "What wonderful scrap they'll make,"
he crowed, scraping his claws together menacingly.

He drove right over to Rod's factory and pounded
on the door.

Rod called out politely, "Who's there?"

CAMERA

1 2

3 4

VIEW

"A neighbor come to welcome you," sang Wolfgang in a silvery voice. He was in a very good mood.

Rod looked at the camera screen. When he saw Wolfgang, his gears seized.

"Mother told me not to let in strangers," Rod called. "Especially you!"

"Now you've hurt my feelings," Wolfgang lied. "Didn't your mother teach you manners? I think you owe someone an apology."

"You're right," said Rod, hanging his head in shame. "That was rude of me." He opened the door.

Quick as a spark, Wolfgang pulled out Rod's batteries and began dismantling the bot.

"These parts will do nicely," he thought. He took them home to his shop and worked through the night.

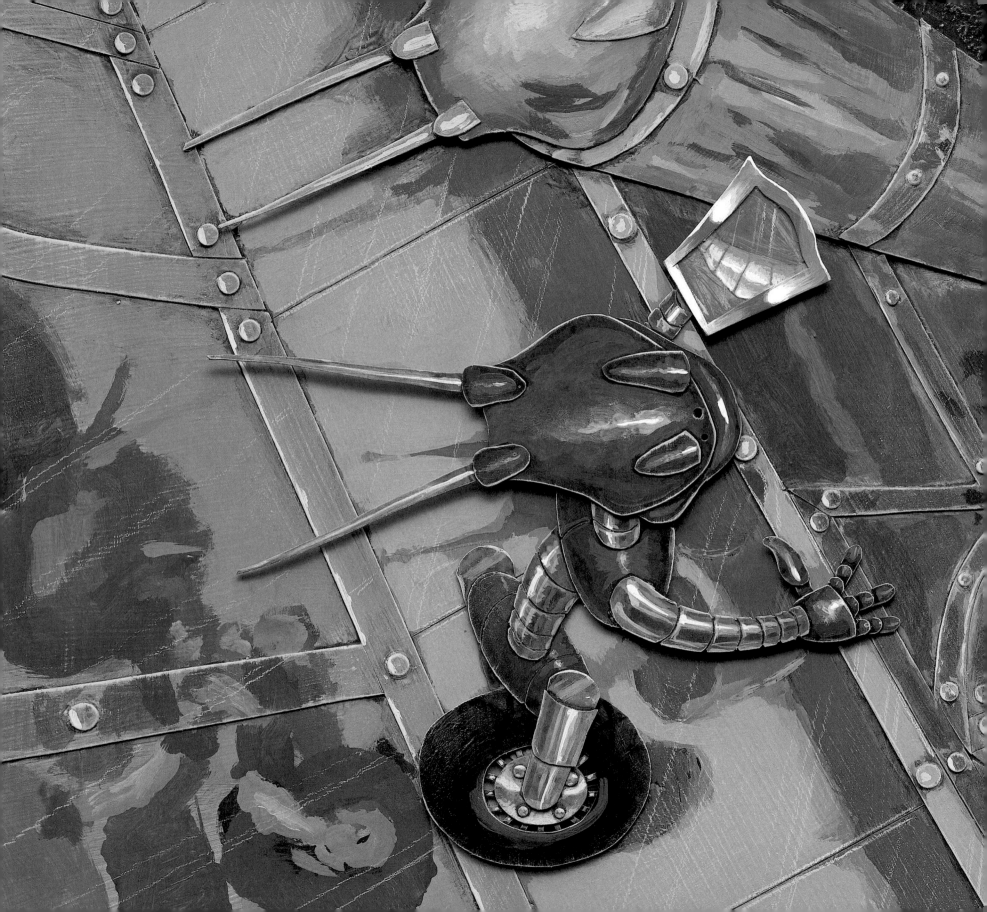

The next day Wolfgang still hungered for more. He wheeled over to the new steel castle, where Slick was posing on the balcony.

"Oooh," thought Wolfgang, grinning toothily, "his parts look imported."

He called up to Slick, "My, you're finely constructed! Let me see you closer."

Wolfgang's voice broke Slick's gaze from the mirrored walls. Slick could not resist an audience.

"Once this trash hound gets a good look at me," he thought as he rode down in the elevator, "he'll know I'm far too outstanding to recycle."

Slick threw open the front door and strutted out. "You may admire me now."

"Hmmm . . . very impressive, but I dunno. Your welding looks a little sloppy, at least from here. And hmmm . . . pity about that rust."

"Are you kidding?" blustered Slick, offended. "I insist you take a closer look!"

Wolfgang rolled in and unplugged Slick with one smooth motion. Slick's lights flickered out.

Wolfgang cackled. "What an ego on that one! This guy has more chrome than a motorcycle!" He hauled Slick back to his shop and broke him down into parts.

Even all of Slick's shiny metal wasn't enough for Wolfgang, though. "Tomorrow morning I'll snag that third one," he mused.

The next morning Dudley was happily wallowing in his pile of mud,
as usual. When Wolfgang arrived, Dud looked up calmly. He had been
expecting him.

"Boy, he looks even dumber than the first two," Wolfgang
thought. "Come over here," he ordered. "I don't want
to get dirt up my tailpipe."

"I'm sorry. Are you talking to me?" asked Dud. "I must have mud in my ears BUZZ BUZZ. You'll have to come closer."

"It's barely worth the trip," Wolfgang complained to himself. "I'm not even sure I can salvage anything good from this one."

Wolfgang drove into the mud, but the bulk of his new upgrades made him heavy and clumsy.

"Argh! I'm slipping!" he exclaimed. "Hey, Rustbucket, can't you come over here?"

"Huh BLIP BUZZ?" said Dud. He almost blew a circuit trying not to giggle. "You look a little steamed. Come on in—the mud is nice and cool BEEP BIP."

"That's it, you dented-up dustbin! I'm gonna get you!" Wolfgang bellowed as he charged forward. But his wheel slid and spun in the mud. The more he thrashed, the deeper he sank.

"Help! I'm stuck! Give me a hand, you pile of scrap!"

"No, I don't think I'll be giving you my hand BUZZ WHIRR—or any other part of me." said Dud, glancing meaningfully at Wolfgang's newest attachments.

"Glub, blub, blub, bl . . . " said Wolfgang.
The mud closed over his head.

In the weeks that followed, Wolfgang rose from the mud in pieces: a deflated tire . . . a rusty claw . . . a crusty gear.

"Now look at this!" said Dud with a heavy sigh. "That big hunk of junk has messed up my perfect mud BUZZ BEEP. And Mom keeps asking about Rod and Slick."

So he went to work.

The next morning Dudley, his brothers, and his mother went out for a family drive. Things were back to normal. . . . Well, almost.